Illustrated by Art Mawhinney

Published by
Louis Weber, C.E.O.
Publications International, Ltd.
7373 North Cicero Avenue
Lincolnwood, Illinois 60712

Ground Floor, 59 Gloucester Place
London W1U 8JJ

Customer Service: 1-800-595-8484 or customer_service@pilbooks.com

www.pilbooks.com

p i kids is a trademark of Publications International, Ltd., and is registered in the United States.
Look and Find is a trademark of Publications International, Ltd.,
and is registered in the United States and Canada.

8 7 6 5 4 3 2 1

Manufactured in USA.

ISBN-10: 1-4508-1877-3
ISBN-13: 978-1-4508-1877-3

Look and Find®

MARVEL STUDIOS

CAPTAIN AMERICA™

THE FIRST AVENGER

pi kids®

publications international, ltd.

Steve Rogers is a small boy, nothing like Captain America. But scrappy Steve has gotten into a scuffle outside a movie theater. Look for his pal Bucky and these other people in the theater and the alley.

Bucky

Steve and Bucky visit The World of Tomorrow, a fair that shows what the future might hold. There are gadgets and contraptions of all kinds, but Steve is only interested in joining the army. While Steve enlists, look for these things that were futuristic for the 1940s.

At long last, Steve Rogers is in the army! He's training under the watchful eyes of Dr. Erskine, Peggy Carter, and Colonel Phillips. The program will determine which recruit will be turned into America's first Super Soldier. Follow Steve through the tough obstacle course and look out for these obstacles.

Selected as the first trial Super Soldier, Steve Rogers is on his way to becoming Captain America! Make your way through the busy and dangerous Rebirth Lab and find this technology that was ahead of its time in the 1940s.

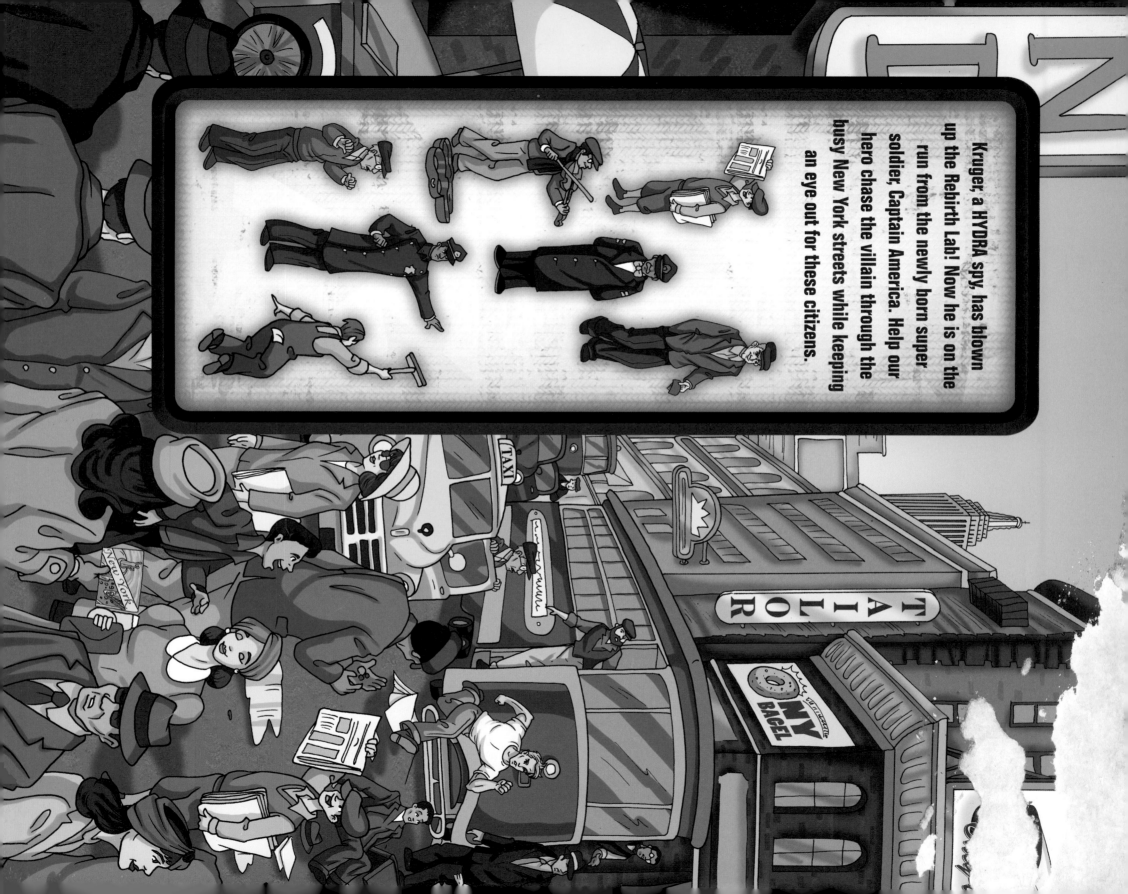

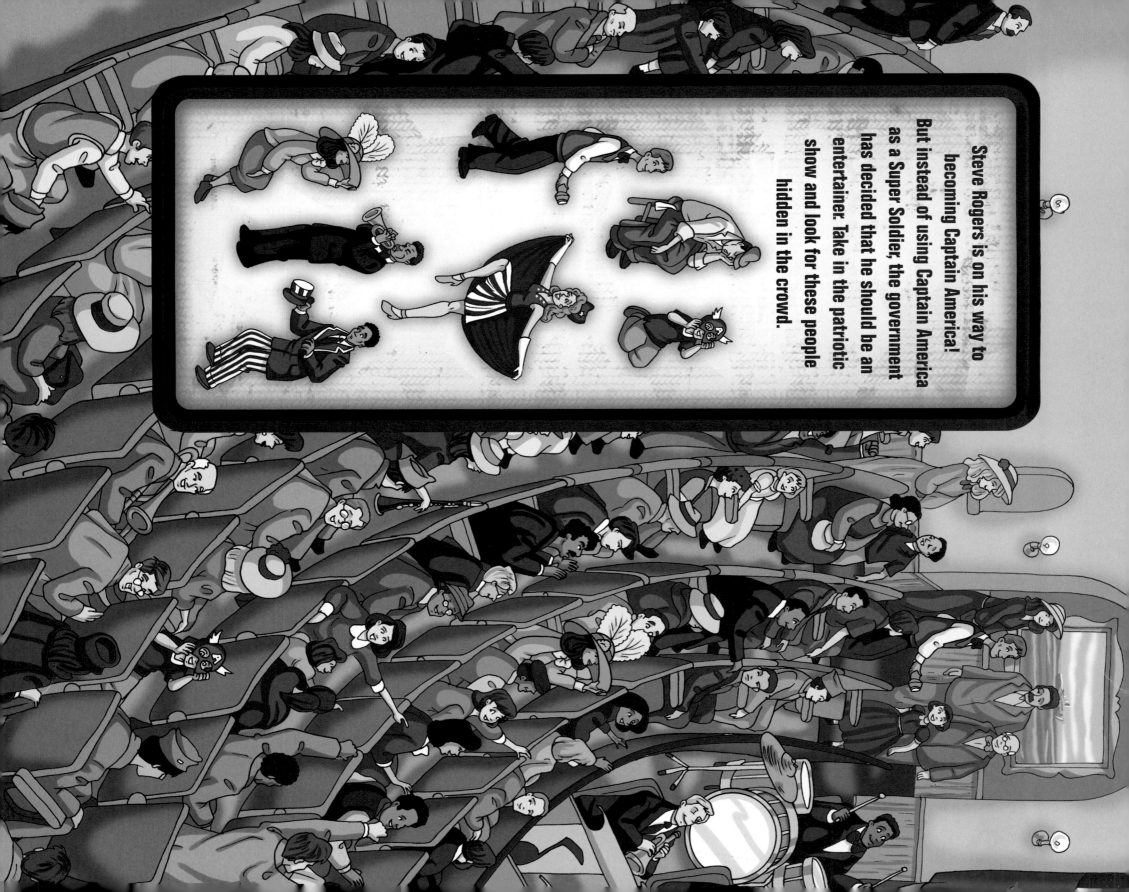

Steve Rogers is on his way to becoming Captain America! But instead of using Captain America as a Super Soldier, the government has decided that he should be an entertainer. Take in the patriotic show and look for these people hidden in the crowd.

Head back to the alley outside the movie theater and look for these historical items hidden around the scene.

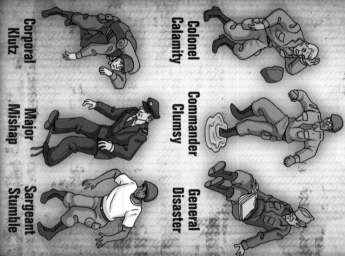

March back to the army training camp and try to spot these soldiers who just aren't cutting it.

Colonel Calamity

Commander Clumsy

General Disaster

Corporal Klutz

Major Mishap

Sargeant Stumble

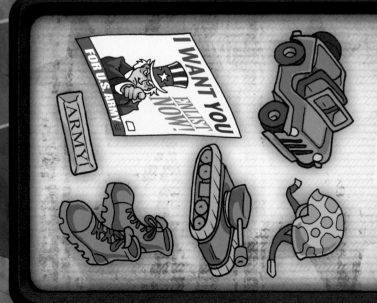

Travel back to The World of Tomorrow and look for these army-related items that caught Steve's patriotic eye.

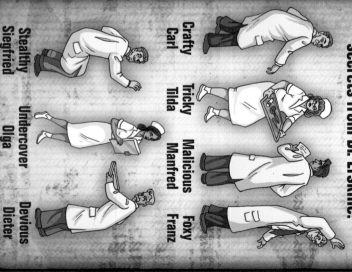

Sneak back into the Rebirth Lab and spy on these villains who are looking to steal the Super Soldier secrets from Dr. Erskine.

Crafty Carl

Tricky Tilda

Malicious Manfred

Foxy Franz

Stealthy Siegfried

Undercover Olga

Devious Dieter

Jitterbug back to Captain America's big show and find these musical items hidden around the theater.

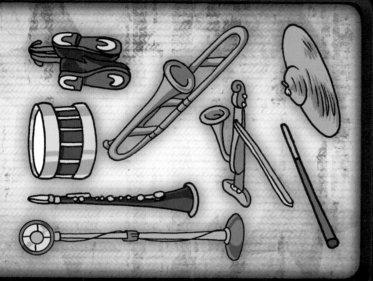

Soar back to the final battle scene and find these explosive devices before they blow up.

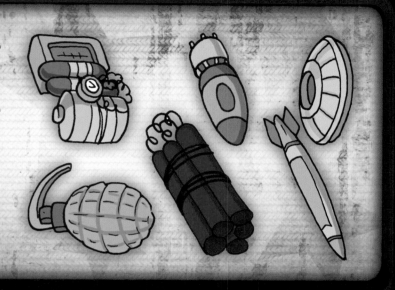

Hurry back to the city streets and find these iconic New York items.

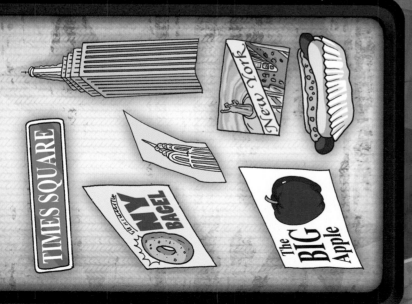

TIMES SQUARE

NY BAGEL

New York

The BIG Apple

Skydive back to the HYDRA factory and identify these characters hidden around the busy scene.

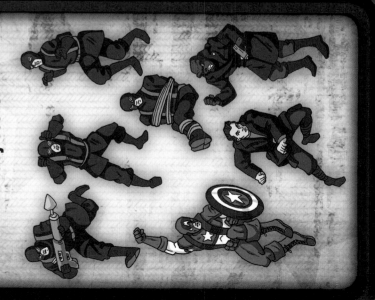